**I'M AN EXPERIENCED HUNTER** of humans. It's not hard, if you understand how they think. People have tunnel vision and are objective-driven. As long as you don't interfere with their goal, and don't make yourself known before you're ready to pounce, you can close in on a relaxed target pretty easily. It doesn't even require much stealth. Unlike animals, human beings don't use their alarm system of senses. Though the wind was behind me, Ben Hammond didn't smell me. He didn't hear my breath over the clunk of his boots on the pavement.

Hammond's objective was his late-model Honda Civic on the edge of the parking lot. So that's all he could see – he didn't notice me round the corner from the loading dock and fall into step behind him. He left the shopping centre with hands full of groceries swinging at his sides and headed across the parking lot, already sliding into the driver's seat in his mind, shutting the door on the moonless night.

I followed with my head down, the hoodie pulled up against the security cameras trained on the few remaining cars. I let him pull his keys out of his pocket, the jangling sound covering the soft fall of my boots for the last few steps between me and my prey.

I closed the distance and attacked.

**'FUCK!' BEN HAMMOND GRABBED** at the back of his head where I'd punched him, turned and stumbled against the car, dropping the bags. Glass cracked in one of them. He cowered in a half-crouch, trying to make himself smaller. Both hands shot up. 'Oh my God! What are you doing?'

'Stand up,' I waved impatiently.

'Take my wallet,' he stammered. 'Don't hurt m—'

'You don't like the surprise attack, do you, Ben? You know how effective it is.'

He realised three things very quickly. First, that I was a woman. Second, that this wasn't a mugging. Third, that he'd heard my voice before.

The man straightened almost fully and squinted into the darkness of my hood. I tugged the hood down and watched his eyes wander around the silhouette of my short hair against the shopping-centre lights, the terror in his face slowly dissipating.

'I . . .' He straightened. His hands dropped. 'I know you.'

'You do.'

'You're that cop.' He pointed an uncertain finger at me, began to shake it as his confidence grew. 'You're that cop from the trial.'

'I am,' I said. 'Detective Harriet Blue, here to deliver your punishment.'

**IT WAS A LITTLE** insulting that my name didn't come to Ben's mind as quickly as I'd hoped. But I had just cracked him on the skull. What little grey matter was sloshing around his brain probably needed time to recover. I'd done everything I could to make him aware of me while he was tried for the rape of his ex-girlfriend Molly. When I took to the stand to testify that I'd found Molly at the bottom of the shower where he'd dumped her, I'd looked right at him and calmly and clearly stated my name.

It hadn't been a solid case. Ben had been very crafty in getting back at his ex for leaving him: raping and beating her, but charming his way into her apartment struggle-free and sharing a glass of wine with her first, so it looked as if she'd welcomed the sexual encounter. I'd known, sitting on the witness stand and staring at him, that like most rapists he'd probably go free.

But that didn't mean I was finished with him.

'This is assault.' Ben touched the back of his head, noted the blood on his fingers and almost smiled. 'You're in a lot of trouble, you stupid little bitch.'

'Actually,' I slid my right foot back, '*you're* in a lot of trouble.'

I gave Ben a couple of sharp jabs to the face, then backed up, let him have a moment to feel them. He stepped out from between the shopping bags and came at me swinging. I sidestepped and planted my knee in his ribs, sending him sprawling on the asphalt. I glanced at the distant shopping centre. The security guards would notice a commotion at the edge of the furthest parking lot camera and come running. I figured I had seconds, not minutes.

'You can't do this.' Hammond spat blood from his split lip. 'You—'

I gave him a knee to the ribs, then lifted him before he could get a lungful of air and slammed him into the bonnet. I'm petite, but I box, so I know how to manoeuvre a big opponent. I grabbed a handful of Ben's hair and dragged him towards the driver's door.

'You're a cop!' Hammond wailed.

'You're right,' I said. I could just make out two security guards rushing out of the loading dock.

'My job gives me access to crime alerts,' I said. 'I can tag a person's file and get a notification every time they're brought in, even if their original charge never stuck.'

I held on to Hammond's hair and gave him a couple of hard punches in the head, then dumped him onto the ground. The guards were closer. I stepped on Hammond's balls, so I knew I had his full attention.

'If I ever see your name in the system again,' I told him, 'I'm coming back. And I won't be this gentle next time.'

I pulled my hood up and sprinted into the scrubland at the side of the lot.

**I'M NOT A VIGILANTE.** Sometimes I just have no choice but to take matters into my own hands.

I'd worked in sex crimes for five years, and I was tired of seeing predators walking free from convictions. When I got close to a victim, the way I did with Molly Finch, I found it hard to sleep after their attacker was acquitted. For weeks I'd lain awake at night thinking about Hammond's smug face as he'd walked down the steps of the courthouse on Goulburn Street, the wink he'd given me as he got into the taxi. I'd managed to make a minor physical assault charge stick. But there had been no proving *beyond a reasonable doubt* that the sex Hammond had had with Molly that night hadn't been consensual.

That's how it goes sometimes with sexual assaults. The guy's lawyer throws everything he has at the idea that she might have wanted it. There was no physical evidence, or witnesses, to say otherwise.

Well, now there was no evidence to say Ben Hammond wasn't bashed half to death by a mugger gone nuts, either. If he went to the cops about what I'd done, he'd know what it felt like not to be believed.

But he wouldn't go to the cops and tell them a woman had given him a beatdown. His kind never did.

I rolled my shoulders as I drove back across the city towards Potts Point, sighing long and low as the tension eased. I was really looking forward to getting some sleep. Most nights saw me at my local gym pounding boxing bags to try to exhaust myself into a healthy pre-sleep calm. Smacking Ben around had given me the same delicious fatigue in my muscles. I hoped it lasted.

At the big intersection near Kings Cross, a pair of hookers strutted across the road in front of my car. Their skin was lit pink by the huge neon Coca-Cola sign on the corner. The streets were still damp from a great storm the night before. The gutters were crowded with trash and huge fig-tree leaves.

My phone rang. I recognised the number as my station chief.

'Hello, Pops,' I said.

'Blue, take down this address,' the old man said. 'There's a body I want you to look at.'

**MURDER WAS HARD WORK,** but Hope had never been afraid of that.

She knelt on the floor of the kitchen of the *Dream Catcher* and scrubbed at the polished boards. She was trying to push her brush down the cracks and bring up the blood that had dried and settled there. *Deck*, she thought suddenly, dunking the brush in the bucket of hot water and bleach beside her. On yachts, the floor was not a floor at all but a deck. The kitchen was called a *galley*. She smiled. She'd need to get used to all the terminology. There was so much to learn, being a new boat owner. She sat back on her heels and wiped the sweat from her brow. She'd give the blood a rest for a while and work on the bedroom.

The young woman climbed backwards down the little ladder and walked into the yacht's expansive bedroom, gathering up a garbage bag from the roll she'd placed on the bed. The first thing she did was take a framed photograph from the nightstand and dump it in the darkness of the bag. She didn't look at the couple's smiling faces. She threw in some reading glasses, a pair of slippers and a folded newspaper. She opened the cupboard and started taking out the woman's clothes, grabbing great handfuls on coat hangers and bundling the shirts, skirts and pants into a roll before she shoved them into the bag.

Jenny Spelling had awful taste, Hope thought, glancing at a turquoise skirt-suit before it went into the trash. Ugh, shoulder pads. So eighties. She felt a wave of excitement roll over her as she looked along the empty hanging pole, thinking about her own clothes racked there.

When she'd filled all the garbage bags on the rolls with their possessions, Hope walked to the back of the boat to check on her prisoners. The couple were slumped in the corner of the shower cubicle, Jenny's head twisted back against the wall so that her nose pointed upward and her mouth hung open. When Hope opened the door, Ken shifted up as much as his binds would allow. His wife was limp against him.

'I'm just heading out to get rid of some rubbish,' Hope said brightly. 'You guys need anything before I go? More water?'

Jenny Spelling woke and immediately started shivering. She stared at Hope wordlessly, as though she didn't know what the young woman was.

'Hope.' Ken's face reddened with desperation. 'I'm begging you, please, just take the boat. Take everything. My wife needs to do her dialysis or she's going to die. OK? It's only going to take a few minutes. That's all. That—'

'We've discussed this.' Hope held up her hand, gave him a weary sigh. 'It'll all be over soon. I'm not getting into this again. The last time I let you loose, you did this.' She held up her forearm, showed him the bruise. '*Trust*, Ken. You had it, and you lost it.'

'Please, please.' Ken shifted. 'You don't need to do this. Look at her. Look at her face. She's missed her dialysis for three days now. She's not right. She's—'

Hope took the duct tape from the counter beside the toilet and ripped off a length. She placed a strip over Jenny's mouth, but gave Ken a few turns around his head. He was the feisty one. She worked emotionlessly as the tape sealed off his words.

'She's gonna die!' the man howled through the tape. 'Please!'

**HEADING TO THE CRIME** scene, I drove through the quiet streets of Picnic Point and up through the national park. The dark hills were spotted here and there with the gold porch lights of suburban mansions. I'd spent some time out here as a pre-teen with one of the foster families who had taken on my brother Sam and me. That is, before their adoption dream had ended.

There had been so many young families who'd attempted to integrate us that it was difficult to decide which one it had been. All I remembered was the local school and the crowds of teens in green and gold uniforms, the curious glances we'd received as we entered midway through the semester.

As usual, Sam and I had only been at the school for a few weeks. As a pair of kids who'd been in the system since we were practically toddlers, we didn't make life easy for our foster parents with our bad behaviour. It was probably me who had broken the spell by running away in the middle of the night. Or maybe it was Sam setting something on fire, or running his mouth at our potential new parents. We'd both been equally bad at school – fighting off kids who wanted to give us grief, trying to show our new teachers who was really boss. Once our new mummies and daddies realised we weren't grateful for being 'saved', the fantasy usually died. In truth, Sam and I had always preferred the group homes and institutions they shipped us to between potential adopters. More places to hide. I dreamed as I drove by the lamplit houses of what it might have been like to grow up here, if I'd been a more stable kid.

The police tape started at the edge of the main road. I was stopped by a young officer in a raincoat and flashed him my badge, only then realising that my knuckles were still wrapped.

'OK, Detective Blue, head down to the end of this road where it turns to dirt and go left along the river. You'll see the lights,' the cop said.

'The river? Shit!' I felt the fine hairs on my arms stand on end. 'Who's the victim?'

The cop waved me on. Another car was coming up behind me. I stood on the gas and zipped down the slope, almost swerving on the corner where the dirt began. I couldn't wait to get to the crime scene. If the victim was a young woman, it meant the Georges River Killer had struck again.

And I was going to get him this time.

**I PARKED CLOSE, UNWRAPPED** my knuckles and strode up to the crime scene with my heart pumping in my ears. I didn't even bring my scene kit. I had to know as much as I could, as fast as possible, so that I could get Pops to put me on the case. The Georges River killings were splashed all over the newspapers, and so were the idiots who had control of the case – a group of loutish guys from Sydney Metro Homicide who wouldn't give me so much as a whiff of what they had.

I didn't want the notoriety these cops seemed to enjoy so much. I wanted to be involved in catching what was probably the most savage serial killer in our nation's history. Young, beautiful university students were going missing from the hip urban suburbs around the University of Sydney campus. Their savaged bodies were turning up on the banks of the Georges River three or four days after they disappeared. My brother spent two days of his working week teaching undergrad design students at the university, and lived in their midst in the hip suburbs around Newtown and Broadway. I'd talked to Sam about it a lot, about how the girls in his apartment building were terrified, begging the landlord to put cameras up outside the block, walking each other to and from their cars in the late hours.

It might have been arrogant, or naive, but I felt as if there was something I could contribute. Though my conviction rate in sex crimes wasn't good, that was part of the culture of the court system. I was a good cop, and I could practically smell the Georges River Killer haunting the women of my city. When the police came knocking on that evil prick's door, I wanted to be right there to see his face.

The first thing I noticed that was wrong with the scene was the edge of the police tape. It was far too crowded. Half the officers who should have been in the inner cordon were standing at the outer cordon, talking and smoking in the dark. I recognised a photographer from my station loitering uselessly by the lights rigged up over the scene. A fingerprints specialist was sitting under a tree eating a burrito out of a paper roll. What the hell was everyone doing? I ducked under the tape and came up beside the only officer in the crime scene. He was crouched over the body.

When he turned around, I saw that the man by the body was Tate Barnes.

The walking embodiment of career suicide.

**THE EFFECT OF SEEING** Tate Barnes right in the middle of what I already considered my crime scene was like being maced. My eyes stung and my throat closed with panic. I'd never met the man before, but I knew the shaggy blond hair and the leather jacket from stories I'd heard. There were hundreds of variations on the story of Tate Barnes. It was a terrible tale about a crime the man had committed that he'd tried to hide from the bosses during his academy application. It was said that, as a child, Tate and a group of his friends had murdered a mother and her young son.

I turned away and grabbed at my face, tried to suppress a groan. I needed this guy out of my crime scene. Now. He straightened and offered me his hand.

'I'm Tox Barnes,' he rasped. It sounded as though his throat was lined with sandpaper.

'You actually introduce yourself as "Tox"?'

'I find it minimises confusion.'

I'd heard the nickname, but I hadn't expected him to embrace it. Officers called Barnes 'Toxic' because any officer who agreed to work with him was essentially committing themselves to a lifetime of punishment from their fellow officers. General consensus was that Tox Barnes should never have been allowed into the force. Those who had worked with him were harassed relentlessly by their peers. He was the fox in the henhouse. Aligning yourself with him meant you were on the side of a predator.

I'd heard that there was nothing the administration had been able to do to stop Barnes being a cop. He'd aced his application, and he'd committed the murders so young his record had been expunged. But that didn't mean the rest of the force was going to sit by and let a murderer operate in their midst. He was the enemy, and if you joined him, you were the enemy too.

'Listen, Tox, I'm Detective Harriet Blue.' I shook his rough hand half-heartedly. 'I'm going to need you to clear out of this scene. Chief Morris has put me on it.'

'Meh,' Tox said, and returned to crouching.

I waited, but nothing further came, so I bent down beside him and glanced at the body.

'Sorry, I didn't catch that.'

'I said "Meh",' Tox replied. 'It was a dismissive noise.'

I was so shocked, so furious, I hadn't even taken in the sight of the girl on the sand before us. My eyes flicked over her naked chest, unseeing, as I tried to get my mind around the reality of the situation. She looked mid-twenties, beautiful, dark-haired. She was wearing only a pair of panties. She was a Georges River girl. I knew it. I needed to get this parasite of a man off my case.

'You don't understand,' I said, 'this is my crime scene. This is my case. And I don't work with partners.'

'Neither do I,' he said, as if it were a matter of choice.

'Right.' I sighed. 'So you can give me a brief on what you've observed, and then I need you to beat it and take your dismissive noises with you.'

Tox seemed to smirk in the dark, stood and walked around the back of the body. I couldn't tell if he'd heard me or not. At the edge of the police tape, twenty yards away, my fellow officers were watching carefully to see if I'd cooperate with their nemesis, thereby giving them permission to make my life a living hell. I noticed some journalists among the crowd. The uniformed patrol officers securing the scene were so interested in Tox and me that they weren't even pushing them back.

When I turned around, I saw that Tox had a pocket knife. He flicked open the blade with a snap, and slashed at the girl.

# A murderer is on the streets.
# All of India is watching.

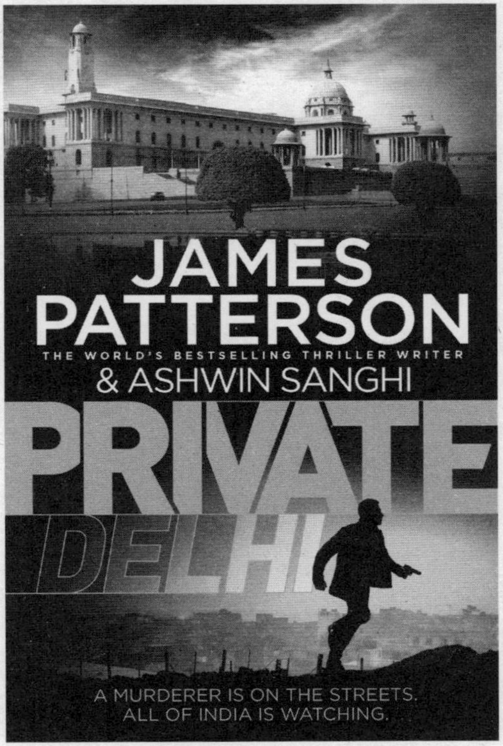


**Read on for an extract**

THE KILLER EMPTIED the final bag of ice into the bath and shut off the cold tap.

With the tub full he stood back to admire his handiwork, watching his breath bloom. Winter in Delhi, it was cold, but the temperature in the small bathroom was even lower than outside and falling fast, just the way he wanted it.

From outside came the sound of footsteps on the stairs and the killer moved quickly. His victim was early but that was fine, he was prepared, and in a heartbeat he left the bathroom and crossed the front room of the apartment, scooping his hypodermic syringe from a table as he passed. A scratching sound announced the key in the lock and the victim opened the door.

The killer attacked from behind, grabbing the victim, pulling him into the room, and smothering a cry of surprise with one gloved hand. He used the syringe and for a second the victim struggled, then went limp. The killer let him drop to the carpet, checked the corridor outside, and then kicked the door shut. He bent to the victim and began to undress him.

Ten minutes later the victim awoke, naked and gasping in the bath. The bathroom light was off and his eyes hadn't yet adjusted to the gloom but he heard the clicking of the ice cubes and knew instantly where he was. His arms had been hoisted overhead, handcuffed to the taps; submerged in the ice, his feet and knees were bound. As he began to struggle he heard someone enter the room and then a gloved hand pushed his head beneath the cubes. He inhaled icy water, feeling his airways fill and his heart constrict with the shock of the sudden cold. When the hand allowed him back to the surface, his coughs and splutters were punctuated by the violent chattering of his teeth.

The figure loomed over him, a shadow in the darkened bathroom. "You'll feel it in your toes and fingertips first," he said. "Tingling. Then numbness. That's your body redirecting resources to protect the vital organs. Clever thing, the body, it can adapt quickly. If you were an Inuit, an Aborigine, even a Tibetan Buddhist monk, then withstanding this kind of cold would be simple for you, but you're not those things, you're . . ."

The killer moved into view. In his hand was the victim's name badge, taken from his shirt. "Rahul," he read, and then tossed it into the bath. "Oh, I do apologize. I'm sure you know all about the effects of cold on the human body. You know all about the slow shutting down of the various functions, how the brain dies before the heart."

"Who are you?" managed Rahul. He squinted. "Do I know you?" The attacker's voice was familiar somehow.

"I don't know," said the attacker. "Do you?" He perched on the edge of the bath and Rahul could see he wore all black, including a black balaclava. Opaque surgical gloves seemed to shine dully in the gloom, giving him the appearance of an evil mime.

"You're wondering why I'm here," said the man, as though reading his thoughts. He smiled and removed from his pocket a tiny little tool that he showed to Rahul. "Are you familiar with a procedure called enucleation?"

JACK MORGAN ENJOYED risk. Why else would he be standing outside this door at 4 a.m., barely daring to breathe as he used a tiny lubricating spray on the lock and then went to work with his pick, nudging interior tumblers into place?

But not blind risk.

Again, that was the reason the owner of the world-renowned Private investigation agency had arrived in Delhi two days earlier than his official schedule predicted, and more discreetly than usual. It was because he liked his risk with a little forethought.

He liked *calculated* risk.

He slid into the darkened apartment like a shadow. From his pocket he took a rubber doorstop, closed the front door as far as he could without making a sound, and then wedged it.

Next he listened. For close to five minutes Jack stood in silence by the door, letting his eyes adjust and taking in the scant furniture—a sofa, a television, an upturned packing crate for a coffee table—but more than anything, listening—listening to the noise that emanated from the bedroom.

What he heard was the sound of a man enduring a fitful sleep, a man who mewled with the pain of nightmares.

Jack trod noiselessly through the apartment. In the kitchen he opened the fridge door and peered inside. Nothing. Back in the front room he went to the upturned crate.

On it stood a bottle of whisky. Johnnie Walker.

*Oh, Santosh*, thought Jack to himself. *Tell me you haven't.*

From the bedroom the sound of Santosh Wagh's nightmares increased, so Jack Morgan finished his work and let himself out of the apartment and into the chill Delhi morning.

IN THE UPMARKET area of Greater Kailash in South Delhi, in a row of homes, a young couple stood at the gate of an abandoned house.

"This is it," said the boy, his breath fogging in Delhi's winter air.

"Are you sure?" asked the girl at his side.

"Sure I'm sure," he replied. "C'mon, let's go inside."

They climbed over the gate easily and made their way through overgrown grass to the front door. Padlocked. But the boy used a pick to crack the lock in less than two minutes. *Not bad for an amateur*, he thought to himself.

He went to open the door, but it wouldn't budge.

"What's wrong?" asked the girl. She was shivering

and cold and desperately wishing they'd decided to go to the cinema instead of opting to make out here.

The boy was puzzled. "I thought it was unlocked . . ."

"What do we do now, then?" said the girl.

Like all young men governed by their libido, the boy wasn't about to give up easily. Yes, it was cold, but he'd come armed with a blanket and the garden was sufficiently overgrown to screen them from the street.

"We don't need to go inside. Let's just stay out here," the boy suggested.

"But it's so cold," she gasped.

"We'll soon warm each other up," he assured her, leading her to an area close to the front of the house. The grass was damp but he covered it with the blanket from his backpack, and the foliage not only screened them but also protected them from the chill breeze. She tried to imagine that they had found themselves a secret garden, and when he produced a spliff, it sealed the deal.

They sat and spent some minutes in relaxed, agreeable silence as they smoked the spliff, listening to the muted sounds of the city drifting to them through the trees. Then they lay down and began kissing. In a few moments they were making love, cocooned in weed-induced sexual bliss.

"What's that?" she said.

"What's what?" he asked, irritated.

"That noise." Then her senses sharpened. "It's the ground. The ground is—"

She didn't get to finish her sentence. Suddenly it was as though the grass were trying to swallow them. Subsidence. A sinkhole. Something. Either way, the earth gave way beneath them, and the two lovebirds crashed through the lawn and into a nightmare beneath.

DAZED, THE GIRL pulled herself to her hands and knees, coughing and gagging at a sudden stench, a mix of caustic chemicals and something else. Something truly stomach-turning.

The floor was rough concrete. She was in a low-ceilinged basement. A gray patch of light in the ceiling indicated where they'd fallen through. Plasterboard, turf, and rotted wooden beams hung down as though in the aftermath of a storm.

And pulling himself up back through the hole was her boyfriend.

"Hey," she called. "Where are you . . . ?"

But he was gone.

Naked, wincing in pain, and consumed with a creeping

sense of something being terribly, terribly wrong, the girl looked around, her eyesight adjusting to the gloom. She saw gas masks and coveralls hanging from pegs. A small chainsaw. Dotted around the concrete floor was a series of plastic barrels with some kind of toxic chemical fumes rising from each one. And even in her traumatized state she realized it was those fumes that had eroded the ceiling structure enough for it to collapse.

And then she saw other things too. They seemed to appear out of the darkness. A table, like a butcher's block, with a huge meat cleaver protruding from the bloodstained wood. And from the plastic barrels protruded hands and feet, the skin bubbling and burning as though being subjected to great heat.

Bile rising, she knew what was happening here. She knew exactly what was happening here.

*A CHARNEL HOUSE*, thought the Commissioner of Police, Rajesh Sharma, when he returned to the office the next day, with the stink of chemicals and decomposition clinging to him. Rarely had he been quite so grateful to leave a crime scene. Those poor bastards who'd had to stay.

The call had come in at around eleven o'clock the night before. A neighbor had heard screaming, looked out, and seen a terrified young woman, her clothes in disarray, running away from the house.

A short while later it was sealed off. The team had been inside for eight hours and would be there for many more days. They had determined the perp was using hydrofluoric acid to dissolve the bodies in plastic tubs.

There was no way of counting how many, but say one for each barrel, that made eleven at least. Quite a death toll. What's more, it didn't take into account any corpses that might already have been disposed of.

But here was the bit that had really taken Sharma by surprise: the house was owned by the Delhi state government.

Mass murder. On government property. He would have to ensure the press did not get hold of this story; in fact, he'd have to make sure the news reached as few ears as possible.

Sharma had washed his hands. He'd rubbed at his face. But he could still smell the corpses as he sat behind his desk at police headquarters and greeted his guest.

The man who took a seat opposite was Nikhil Kumar, the Honorable Minister for Health and Family Welfare. Photoshoot-perfect, not a strand of jet-black hair out of place, Kumar wore simple khaki slacks, an Egyptian cotton shirt, a Canali blazer, and comfortable soft-leather loafers. His very presence made Sharma feel overweight and scruffy by comparison. Well, let's face it, he *was* overweight and scruffy. But Kumar made him feel even more so.

"What can I do for you, sir?" Sharma asked the minister. It paid to be courteous to ministers.

"Thank you for seeing me at such short notice," said Kumar.

"I'm happy to help. What's on your mind?"

"I am given to understand that your men searched a house in Greater Kailash today. I was wondering if you could share some information regarding what you found."

Sharma tried not to let his irritation show as he considered his response. On the one hand he wanted to keep Kumar sweet; on the other, experience had taught him that it was always better to keep politicians out of police inquiries.

"How about you tell me what your interest in this matter is?" he said. "And how you found out about it?"

"As I'm sure you're about to remind me, I have no jurisdiction with the police. You and I stand on the battlements of two opposing forts in the same city. But I have contacts, and I find out what I can. You want to prevent leaks, run a tighter ship."

Sharma chortled. "This is your way of buttering me up, is it, Minister? Coming into my office and criticizing the way I run my police force?"

"Let me be frank with you," said Kumar. "It may not be wise to delve too deeply into this case."

"Minister, we've got at least eleven potential murders here." He was about to reveal he knew the building was owned by the state but stopped himself, deciding to keep his powder dry. "While I appreciate the need for discretion, we will be delving as deeply as we need to in order to discover the truth."

"Suffice to say that you would be adequately compensated," said Kumar.

Sharma was taken aback. "For what?"

"For your cooperation."

Sharma sat back and made Kumar wait for a response. "I tell you what, Minister—you leave now, and I'll think about your offer."

Sharma watched with satisfaction as Kumar stood and tried to leave the office with as much dignity as he could regain.

Only when the door had closed did Sharma allow himself a smile. This was what they called an opportunity. And when life gives you lemons . . .

SANTOSH WAGH OPENED the front door of his home to find Jack Morgan on the doorstep.

"Santosh!" said Jack, and before Santosh could react he had stepped inside.

As ever, Santosh was happy to see his boss. The thing with Jack was that as soon as he appeared, whatever the time, whatever the place, you were simply a guest in his world. It was impossible not to feel reassured by it. It wasn't just the gun Jack carried; it wasn't just the fact that Jack was enormously wealthy and could boast powerful and high-profile friends. It was just Jack, being Jack.

"Welcome to my humble abode," said Santosh. Looking around, he saw his living quarters through Jack's eyes: hardly furnished, dark, and a little fusty. "I would give you a tour, but I believe you know your way around already."

"I don't follow," said Jack quizzically.

"Years ago when you hired me you told me you thought I was an exceptional detective. Did you really think you could break into my apartment and I wouldn't notice?"

Jack relaxed, allowing himself a smile. The game was up. "Well, I'm an exceptional cat burglar, so I played the odds. How did you know?"

Santosh's cane clicked on the wooden floor as he made his way to the kitchen and then returned with a bottle of whisky that he placed on his makeshift table. He pointed to the bottle with the tip of his cane. "Perhaps you'd like to check it."

Jack leaned forward, holding Santosh's gaze as he reached for the bottle, inverted it, and studied the almost invisible mark he had made with a small bar of hotel soap two nights before.

"It's just as it was the other night," he said, replacing the bottle. "And I'm pleased to see it."

Santosh blinked slowly. "Not nearly as pleased as I am."

"I had to check, Santosh. I had to know."

"You could have asked me."

"But addicts lie. That's what they do. Besides, why even have it in the house if you don't plan to drink it?"

The answer was that Santosh preferred to face temptation head-on. He would spend hours just staring at the bottle. It was for that reason, not his renowned detective skills, that he had seen the soap mark, and having spotted it he'd studied his front-door lock and detected the odor of lubricant. One phone call to Private HQ later and his suspicions had been confirmed.

Jack had been checking up on him.

But of course he couldn't blame Jack for that. Private was the world's biggest investigation agency, with offices in Los Angeles, London, Berlin, Sydney, Paris, Rio, Mumbai, and, most recently, Delhi. Jack had invested a huge amount of faith in Santosh by making him Private's chief of operations in India.

Santosh had been an agent with the Research and Analysis Wing, India's external intelligence agency, when investigations into the 2006 Mumbai train blasts had brought him into contact with Jack. It had been only a matter of time before he'd recruited Santosh to establish Private in Mumbai. Setting up Private's office in Mumbai had been challenging; his last case had almost killed him and at the very least it had looked as though he might have lost his ongoing battle with the bottle.

Jack had come to his rescue by persuading him to go to rehab, the Cabin in Thailand. Six months later, Jack had persuaded Santosh to move to Delhi to establish Private in the capital.

So Jack had to know that Santosh was still in control of his addiction. And he was. The bottle of whisky had hung around his home untouched for the whole three months he'd been there. Every day Santosh had resisted the temptation to open it and banish his private pain. And every day it got a little easier.

Privately, though, he worried if he could truly operate without it. He worried that his brain might not be able to make the same leaps of logic it once had; he worried that kicking the booze might make him a worse detective, not a better one. These were just a few of the things keeping him awake at night.

"I don't drink it," he told Jack. "That's the important thing."

JACK LOVED TO drive in Delhi. First of all he always made sure to hire an old car, one that already had its fair share of bumps and scrapes, and then he'd climb in, wind down the window, and plunge headlong into the sheer mayhem of one of his favorite cities.

He liked to drive fast. Or at least as fast as he dared, leaning on the horn like a local and winding his way through lines of buses, scooters, cyclists, and auto rickshaws, past glass-fronted buildings and ancient temples, broken-down housing and luxury hotels with glove-wearing staff at the gates. Delhi was a vibrant, colorful mix of cultures old and new. A genuine melting pot. To Jack it felt as though Delhi's entire history—Hindu Rajputs,

Muslim Mughals, and Christian Englishmen—all came to him through the open window of the car, and he breathed it all in—good and bad—breathing its very essence.

At times like that, Jack felt most alive. Blessed. He thought that being Jack Morgan in Delhi was just about the best thing you could be in this world.

Usually, that is.

But not today. Because one thing stronger than his love for driving fast through Delhi was his respect for Santosh Wagh. It was in a car accident that the investigator had lost his wife and child, Isha and Pravir. So, for that reason, Jack drove slowly, with the window closed.

As they made their way through the streets Jack cast a sideways glance at his passenger, a man he was proud to call a friend.

In his early fifties, Santosh looked older than his age. Sleep deprivation and alcohol abuse had taken their toll. His salt-and-pepper stubble was more salt than pepper and the brown wool jacket with leather patches at the elbows gave him the look of a university professor. His eyeglasses were unfashionable and his scarf should have been replaced years earlier. Not that he seemed to care. Aloof and cerebral, permanently ruminative, Santosh was far too preoccupied to care about such trivial matters.

"Tell me about Delhi's political makeup," Jack asked

him, more to keep his passenger's mind off the journey than genuine ignorance on his part.

Santosh cleared his throat. "Delhi's a strange place. It's not only a state in the Indian federation but also India's capital—like Washington, DC. The city's government is split down the middle: civic administration is managed by the Chief Minister, Mohan Jaswal, while law and order is managed by the Lieutenant Governor, Ram Chopra."

Jack slowed to allow a pair of motorbikes to pass, and then immediately regretted it when a cab and an auto rickshaw nipped in front of him as well. *Any other day* . . . he thought ruefully.

"The Chief Minister and the Lieutenant Governor. Do they see eye to eye?" he asked Santosh.

"Jaswal and Chopra?" mused Santosh. "Do they see eye to eye? Now there's a good question. Before I answer it, how about you tell me which one of them we're due to meet."

Jack laughed. He loved to see Santosh's mind working. "I tell you what, my brainy friend. How about *you* tell *me* what the beef is all about, and then I'll tell you which one we're due to see."

"Very well," said Santosh. "The answer to your question is no, Jaswal and Chopra do not see eye to eye. As Chief Minister and Lieutenant Governor respectively, they're supposed to run Delhi in partnership, but the fact of the matter is they agree on nothing.

There is what you might call a difference of opinion when it comes to interpreting the rules of their partnership."

"They hate each other?"

"Pretty much. A jurisdictional war is not the best path to a lasting friendship."

"One of them would dearly like to put one over on the other?"

"As a means of wresting complete control, no doubt." Santosh flinched slightly as a pedestrian passed too close to their car. "Now, how about you tell me which one it is?"

"Chief Minister Mohan Jaswal."

Santosh nodded. "Has he told you why?"

"Nope. Just that he wants to meet. He asked for both of us. What do you know about him?"

"Jaswal started his career with the army and was part of the Indian Peace Keeping Force sent to Sri Lanka in 1987. He opted for early retirement upon his return—traumatized at seeing Tamil Tigers blowing themselves up with explosives strapped to their chests.

"He then became a journalist for the *Indian Times* in Mumbai, working as the newspaper's senior correspondent in New York. A plum posting that most would have coveted. But not Jaswal. He returned to India to enter the political arena, claiming he wanted to 'make a difference.'

"We were acquainted in the days when he was a

journalist and I was with the Research and Analysis Wing. He used to try to pump me for information."

"Were you friendly?"

Santosh looked at Jack. "I didn't particularly trust him, if that's what you mean."

THE CHIEF MINISTER'S Residence at Motilal Nehru Marg occupied over three acres of Delhi's prime real estate, a sprawling white-stuccoed bungalow reminiscent of the colonial era, surrounded by sweeping lawns.

Santosh and Jack stepped out of the battered Fiat and into the cold Delhi air, where Jaswal's secretary waited for them. They were whisked inside without any of the usual security checks, and then ushered into a book-lined study where the Chief Minister, Mohan Jaswal, sat behind his desk.

Now in his early sixties, Jaswal had a youthful vigor that belied his age. He had not an ounce of fat on his body and he sported a neatly trimmed white mustache.

His crisp white kurta pajama and sky-blue turban indicated his Sikh faith.

"Good to meet you, Mr. Morgan," he said, and the two men shook hands.

"Just Jack is fine."

And then to Santosh, Jaswal said, "It's been years."

"I know," replied Santosh curtly.

There was an awkward moment between the two acquaintances, broken only when Jaswal invited them to sit. Tea was served and more pleasantries exchanged: yes, it was cold outside; yes, Jack Morgan had been to Delhi many times before; yes, he was delighted to set up a bureau in the city; no, Santosh had not lived here for very long. Just three months.

All the while the two men from Private sipped their Kashmiri tea, answered Jaswal's questions politely, and waited for him to get to the point of the meeting.

"I need you to handle an exceptionally delicate matter," the Chief Minister said at last.

They waited for him to continue as he took a puff from a bronchodilator. "I hear news of a gruesome discovery at a house in Greater Kailash," he said. "Any more than that, however, is being kept a secret from me."

Questions forming, Jack leaned forward before stopping himself and sitting back to watch Santosh take the lead.

"What sort of gruesome discovery?" asked Santosh,

thanking Jack with the merest incline of his head. His hands were knotted together on the head of his cane; his heart beat just that tiny bit faster. Ushered in to see the Chief Minister, he'd wondered if this might turn out to be a dry, political request. Evidently not.

"Bodies," sniffed Jaswal. "Up to a dozen of them, in various states of . . . decomposition. It seems they were being melted down in some way."

"Some kind of corrosive involved?"

"It would seem that way. Body parts were found in thick barrels full of the stuff."

Jack shifted forward. He and Santosh exchanged a look. "What sort of barrels?" asked Santosh.

"Plastic, as far as I'm aware," said Jaswal.

"Hydrofluoric acid," Santosh and Jack said in unison. Even Santosh allowed himself a thin smile at that one.

"That's significant, is it?" asked Jaswal, looking from one to the other.

"Very," said Santosh. "It tells us that whoever is responsible is concerned firstly with hiding the identity of the victims and secondly with disposing of the corpses. In that specific order. Which means that the identity of the victims is extremely important."

Jaswal raised an eyebrow. "Isn't that always the case?"

"Not at all. For many serial killers the process of killing is what defines the act; the choice of victim can be random, based only on the ability to fulfill that need.

It's what often makes them so hard to catch." He threw a look at Jaswal. "What's your particular interest in this discovery? Over and above curiosity."

"The house in which this . . . grisly operation was discovered is government property."

"And yet you're not being given any information?"

"It wouldn't be the first time."

For a moment or so, Santosh seemed to be lost in his thoughts before he collected himself and addressed Jaswal once more. "Do you believe Ram Chopra is the one suppressing information?"

Jaswal shot Santosh a wintry smile. "What do *you* think?"

"What I think is irrelevant. It's what you think that is important."

"Point taken. And the answer is yes, I do."

"Why?"

"That's one of the things I'd like you to find out."

"Of course. But let me rephrase the question. Why *might* Ram Chopra want to keep you in the dark regarding the discovery at Greater Kailash?"

"Possibly to wrong-foot me, make me appear ill-informed. Possibly something more."

"How did you find out about the bodies?" Jack asked.

"Police tip-off," said Jaswal. "Nobody directly involved with the case. I'm afraid you'll be on your own with this one."

Santosh looked at Jaswal, knowing that if Private

accepted this job then Jack would jet off and it would be he, Santosh, who entered the lion's den.

Santosh was intrigued. Bodies. Hidden motives. It would be messy. Just the way he liked it.

On the other hand, there was something about the case that troubled him. But he couldn't pin down what it was.

## Also by James Patterson

### ALEX CROSS NOVELS

Along Came a Spider • Kiss the Girls • Jack and Jill • Cat and Mouse • Pop Goes the Weasel • Roses are Red • Violets are Blue • Four Blind Mice • The Big Bad Wolf • London Bridges • Mary, Mary • Cross • Double Cross • Cross Country • Alex Cross's Trial (*with Richard DiLallo*) • I, Alex Cross • Cross Fire • Kill Alex Cross • Merry Christmas, Alex Cross • Alex Cross, Run • Cross My Heart • Hope to Die • Cross Justice • Cross the Line

### THE WOMEN'S MURDER CLUB SERIES

1st to Die • 2nd Chance (*with Andrew Gross*) • 3rd Degree (*with Andrew Gross*) • 4th of July (*with Maxine Paetro*) • The 5th Horseman (*with Maxine Paetro*) • The 6th Target (*with Maxine Paetro*) • 7th Heaven (*with Maxine Paetro*) • 8th Confession (*with Maxine Paetro*) • 9th Judgement (*with Maxine Paetro*) • 10th Anniversary (*with Maxine Paetro*) • 11th Hour (*with Maxine Paetro*) • 12th of Never (*with Maxine Paetro*) • Unlucky 13 (*with Maxine Paetro*) • 14th Deadly Sin (*with Maxine Paetro*) • 15th Affair (*with Maxine Paetro*)

### DETECTIVE MICHAEL BENNETT SERIES

Step on a Crack (*with Michael Ledwidge*) •
Run for Your Life (*with Michael Ledwidge*) •
Worst Case (*with Michael Ledwidge*) •
Tick Tock (*with Michael Ledwidge*) •
I, Michael Bennett (*with Michael Ledwidge*) •
Gone (*with Michael Ledwidge*) •
Burn (*with Michael Ledwidge*) •
Alert (*with Michael Ledwidge*) •
Bullseye (*with Michael Ledwidge*)

## NYPD RED SERIES

NYPD Red (*with Marshall Karp*) •
NYPD Red 2 (*with Marshall Karp*) •
NYPD Red 3 (*with Marshall Karp*) •
NYPD Red 4 (*with Marshall Karp*)

## PRIVATE NOVELS

Private (*with Maxine Paetro*) • Private London (*with Mark Pearson*) • Private Games (*with Mark Sullivan*) • Private: No. 1 Suspect (*with Maxine Paetro*) • Private Berlin (*with Mark Sullivan*) • Private Down Under (*with Michael White*) • Private L.A. (*with Mark Sullivan*) • Private India (*with Ashwin Sanghi*) • Private Vegas (*with Maxine Paetro*) • Private Sydney (*with Kathryn Fox*) • Private Paris (*with Mark Sullivan*) • The Games (*with Mark Sullivan*) • Private Delhi (*with Ashwin Sanghi*)

## ROMANCE

Sundays at Tiffany's (*with Gabrielle Charbonnet*) •
The Christmas Wedding (*with Richard DiLallo*) •
First Love (*with Emily Raymond*)

## NON-FICTION

Torn Apart (*with Hal and Cory Friedman*) •
The Murder of King Tut (*with Martin Dugard*)

## OTHER TITLES

Miracle at Augusta (*with Peter de Jonge*)

## FAMILY OF PAGE-TURNERS

### MIDDLE SCHOOL BOOKS

The Worst Years of My Life (*with Chris Tebbetts*) • Get Me Out of Here! (*with Chris Tebbetts*) • My Brother Is a Big, Fat Liar (*with Lisa Papademetriou*) • How I Survived Bullies, Broccoli, and Snake Hill (*with Chris Tebbetts*) • Ultimate Showdown (*with Julia Bergen*) • Save Rafe! (*with Chris Tebbetts*) • Just My Rotten Luck (*with Chris Tebbetts*) • Dog's Best Friend (*with Chris Tebbetts*)

### I FUNNY SERIES

I Funny (*with Chris Grabenstein*) • I Even Funnier (*with Chris Grabenstein*) • I Totally Funniest (*with Chris Grabenstein*) • I Funny TV (*with Chris Grabenstein*)

### TREASURE HUNTERS SERIES

Treasure Hunters (*with Chris Grabenstein*) • Danger Down the Nile (*with Chris Grabenstein*) • Secret of the Forbidden City (*with Chris Grabenstein*) • Peril at the Top of the World (*with Chris Grabenstein*)

### HOUSE OF ROBOTS SERIES

House of Robots (*with Chris Grabenstein*) • Robots Go Wild! (*with Chris Grabenstein*) • Robot Revolution (*with Chris Grabenstein*)

### OTHER ILLUSTRATED NOVELS

Kenny Wright: Superhero (*with Chris Tebbetts*) • Homeroom Diaries (*with Lisa Papademetriou*) • Jacky Ha-Ha (*with Chris Grabenstein*) • Word of Mouse (*with Chris Grabenstein*)

## MAXIMUM RIDE SERIES

The Angel Experiment • School's Out Forever • Saving the World and Other Extreme Sports • The Final Warning Max • Fang • Angel • Nevermore • Forever

## CONFESSIONS SERIES

Confessions of a Murder Suspect (*with Maxine Paetro*) • The Private School Murders (*with Maxine Paetro*) • The Paris Mysteries (*with Maxine Paetro*) • The Murder of an Angel (*with Maxine Paetro*)

## WITCH & WIZARD SERIES

Witch & Wizard (*with Gabrielle Charbonnet*) • The Gift (*with Ned Rust*) • The Fire (*with Jill Dembowski*) • The Kiss (*with Jill Dembowski*) • The Lost (*with Emily Raymond*)

## DANIEL X SERIES

The Dangerous Days of Daniel X (*with Michael Ledwidge*) • Watch the Skies (*with Ned Rust*) • Demons and Druids (*with Adam Sadler*) • Game Over (*with Ned Rust*) • Armageddon (*with Chris Grabenstein*) • Lights Out (*with Chris Grabenstein*)

## GRAPHIC NOVELS

Daniel X: Alien Hunter (*with Leopoldo Gout*) • Maximum Ride: Manga Vols. 1–9 (*with NaRae Lee*)